KU-360-663

First published in 2014 by Curious Fox, an imprint of Capstone Global Library Limited, 7 Pilgrim Street, London, EC4V 6LB – Registered company number: 6695582

www.curious-fox.com

Copyright © 2013 Capstone Young Readers

The author's moral rights are hereby asserted.

Designer: Russell John Griesmer
All characters in this publication are fictitious and any resemblance to real persons, living or dead, is purely coincidental.

ISBN 978 1 782 02126 1
18 17 16 15 14
10 9 8 7 6 5 4 3 2 1

A CIP catalogue for this book is available from the British Library.

All rights reserved. No part of this publication may be reproduced in any form or by any means (including photocopying or storing it in any medium by electronic means and whether or not transiently or incidentally to some other use of this publication) without the written permission of the copyright owner.

Printed and bound in China